THREE ACES FROM SATAN'S HAND

Bill D. Allen
&
Sherri Dean

Copyright © 2013 Bill D. Allen & Sherri Dean

All rights reserved.

"Tinker's Damn" Appeared in SCIENCE FICTION TRAILS,
Pirate Dog Press, 2007

"Clay Allison and the Haunted Head" Appeared in
SIXGUNS STRAIGHT FROM HELL
Science Fiction Trails Publishing, 2010

ISBN: 1492717983
ISBN-13: 978-1492717980

DEDICATION

This book is dedicated to Paul "Bill" Walls

CONTENTS

Acknowledgments

1 Tinker's Damn   Page 1

2 Clay Allison and the Haunted Head   Page 17

3 Annie Oakley and the Terror of the   Page 34
   World Fair

ACKNOWLEDGMENTS

The authors would like to take the opportunity to thank David B. Riley who bought our first weird western story and set us on the path to this trilogy of oddities.

TINKER'S DAMN

Will Sinclair slumped forward on his saddle, tipped up his big brimmed hat and gazed toward Capulin Mountain on the horizon and a line of dark clouds coming in from the West. He dug in his vest for his pocket watch, checked the time, and snapped open the back to look at the mechanism. He stared at the perfect inner workings of the gears and the hypnotizing motion of the main spring.

"Willie! Willie Sinclair! Wake yer ass up, boy!" Clem Masters hollered.

Will cursed himself for daydreaming. He looked toward the Trail Boss and saw him waving at a young heifer that had taken off from the rest of the herd.

"I see her!" he yelled back. Will wheeled his horse around and lit out for the stray.

Clem's voice called out after him." You got another two days of work, boy. We ain't at Trinidad yet!" Laughter echoed after Will as he chased the stray.

The heifer had wandered into a dry riverbed by the time he caught up. Will carefully guided his horse around to a cut out in the bank and followed. The clouds were rolling in and bringing with them the beginnings of a storm. The wind gusted and kicked up dust from the river bed. Will squinted to see and pulled the bandanna from around his neck up over his mouth and nose to keep from eating dirt.

The sky rapidly darkened as he rushed toward the wayward heifer. She glared at him with wide eyes and spooked, running away from her pursuer.

"Damn it!"

The wind stung his cheeks with its hot, dry touch. Dust clouds billowed and blew closer.

Will got near enough to get a rope around the stray and he looped the lariat around his saddle horn and the heifer jerked to a halt and bellowed in protest. The animal gave some token resistance then gave up the fight.

The storm edged closer. Dust storms were unpredictable. Some blew out in a matter of seconds; some blew down whole towns with their whirling devil dervishes and lasted for days. This one looked like it might take a while. He weighed his options. Will doubted he could make it back to the main herd before the storm hit so he looked around for a place to wait it out. He was damn sure gonna get them out of that riverbed. Flash flood was another danger in this normally dry country.

Will spoke to his horse, calming the mare as she shifted nervously from hoof to hoof. He coaxed both the horse and heifer out of the riverbed and over to shelter of a small nearby mesa and dismounted.

The storm hit like a great howling beast with tiny biting mouths made of stinging sand. Will flinched as a bright bolt of lightning struck some nearby scrub brush. He pressed his hat down and tightened its cord around his chin, then took off his duster and loosely draped it over the horse's head for protection. It had a calming effect. The mare stopped fidgeting around enough for Will to lean against her and use her body to protect his.

The sky turned solid dirt brown with occasional bright flashes of lightning that cracked and popped. The wind whipped brush past him and roared as if angry it couldn't get at him. Will listened and began to hear a new sound just under the storm—a rhythmic chugging like the big trains that ran from Kansas City he'd once seen as a boy. Add in tinkling bells and clanging pots and Will was truly confounded. What could it be?

He squinted into the daytime darkness and saw two round beacons of light cut through the dust from a ways away. It came a little closer, spinning and sputtering gravel in its wake. It looked like a horse, but bigger than he'd ever seen, made of dark cast iron bound with silver rivets and snorting steam from its brass nostrils. It pulled a large covered wagon fearlessly in the midst of the dust storm.

Will wondered if he was dreaming.

The horse was moving faster that he thought possible. It didn't gallop so much as glide bumpily across the ground. It moved closer, then veered to avoid the creek bed and Will got a better look at the wagon.

Colorful flapping bunting whipped against pots and pans tied all around the sideboards. If the storm hadn't been so bad he might have been able to read all the signs on the wagon. As it was he could only make out the words *Herr Professor Urhwerk's Marvels and Medicine Show* in what, on a clear day, would be a garishly painted sign.

He'd be damned if there wasn't some kinda of metal windmill contraption sprouting from the top of the wagon. Fierce living lightning raced across the face of the windmill like blue fire.

The wagon turned north and bumped away into the heart of the dust storm. The heavy canvas curtain on the rear parted and revealed something that made Will's breath stop in this throat.

A beautiful young woman peered from the safety of the wagon. Her face was as perfect as a store bought china doll. Through the dusty air her sapphire bright eyes met Will's and she smiled and winked. The dust kicked up as her graceful hand stretched out in a wave and she disappeared, swallowed by the storm. The wagon rolled away seemingly taking the storm with it.

As the dust died down Will thought about what he'd seen. Who was she? Was she even real, this angel in the wagon from hell? Her eyes haunted him.

His horse nosed him gently and brought him back from his reverie. Will retrieved his duster, shook off the dust and put it back on. Then he mounted up and caught back up with the herd with the heifer in tow.

He made good time and was relieved to see everyone safe although plenty dusty and dirty. Will rode right up to Clem and told him everything—the devil horse, the mysterious wind wagon but mostly about the beautiful woman who'd winked at him.

"Willie boy, you have gone plumb loco," Clem said with a grin. "Them dust devils been playin' tricks on you. With any luck we'll be at the railhead day after tomorrow and you can spend your money on a real woman—not some dusty dream girl."

❖

Will patted his breast pocket and was reassured by the bulge of his money pouch. He'd done the same thing ten times in as many minutes. He needed to stop it. He could hear Clem Master's voice in his mind telling him he was advertising where he kept his money to every thief in the county.

Will said farewell to the cattle drive at Trinidad. Instead of staying with the rest of the men, tearing up the town and spending all their pay together, Will headed back South. Clem had actually cracked a warm smile when he paid Will his earnings. "You're a good man." That's all he said and shook his hand. It meant a lot to Will.

Swede, the cook had even given him a big sack of jerked beef and biscuits to take with him. Will was so touched he didn't have the heart to ask the man how he was supposed to tell the difference.

He left with a touch of sadness, but a passel more of excitement at the prospect of beginning a new life.

Happily he was allowed to take Nell, his favorite mare from the *remuda* and the first thing he intended on doing was chasing down the girl from the strange medicine wagon. He'd been thinking about that girl ever since he saw her. She'd waved at him and smiled, hadn't she? Surely she did. She must have liked the looks of him.

What was she doing in the back of that contraption? No matter how he ciphered it, she flat didn't belong. It was all mighty peculiar, that much was for certain.

He'd been pondering what he'd do once he left the trail. Would he keep heading North, or maybe West to California? He didn't have anything to go back to in Texas. The farm was long gone. His father had died when he was a toddler. His brother James had been lost in the war and his mother had held until Will had grown enough to make it on his own before she finally died of grief. Maybe a girl like her wouldn't mind spending some time with a man like him. Maybe she was tired of eating trail dust and was interested in going to California with him.

He knew he was dreaming. She probably waved at every cowboy just to sell more snake oil. But no matter what, he was determined to locate Professor Uhrwerk's Traveling Show and at least talk to that girl before he did anything else.

He'd stopped off in Cimarron at Lambert's Saloon. It was the one place that everyone passed through on their way anywhere in this part of the country be they cowboy, outlaw or lawman. Someone would surely have heard news of the Professor there.

Lambert's Saloon was a two story, flat roofed building near a stable and a flour mill along the river. He'd heard it was a wild place, but he hoped that since it was early enough perhaps he'd be able to avoid trouble. Just in case he patted the form of the heavy Navy Colt at his hip. He wasn't very fast, but he was accurate when he needed to be. Shoot well or shoot often, his brother James had told him once long ago.

He tied off the reins to the hitching post out front and stepped onto the covered porch. He could hear music coming from within and the smell of surprisingly good food was wafting into the twilight air.

There weren't many people in the saloon. There were some older men playing roulette over on one side of the room, a piano player, and there was a fancy looking character with an eye-patch sitting alone at a Faro table shuffling a deck of cards.

There was a short, soft looking man with a beard tending bar who greeted him as he entered. From what Will had heard about the place, he recognized him as the proprietor Henri Lambert. Supposedly he had been President Lincoln's chef before he headed west.

Henri looked up from polishing the bar and gave Will a wide grin. "Hello there, son. What can I get for you?"

"I'll take a shot of rye," Will said.

The man poured and handed him the drink. "Do you want the bottle?"

Will shook his head. "No, thank you. I don't reckon that would be a good idea. Your name is Lambert, ain't it?"

"*Oui.* Yes. I'm the owner."

"I was told by Clem Masters that you would probably be able to tell me whatever I needed to know."

"Ah, yes, Clem. He hasn't been around in a few years. Probably for the best. Last night Clay Allison was in here dancing naked on the bar. I doubt Clem would much care for that and I don't need any more holes in my roof."

Will glanced up and saw a number of dark holes punched through the pressed tin ceiling.

"I see."

"How do you know Clem Masters?"

"Trail Boss. I rode with him up the Goodnight Trail to the railhead at Trinidad."

He nodded. "You aren't looking for trouble, are you?" Henri asked. It seemed like he was almost pleading with him. "I've had the undertaker drag more than one young cowboy out of here and I don't like seeing it happen. Bad for business."

"No, nothing like that. I just need to know if you know where I might find Professor Uhrwerk's Medicine Show. I know he came through recently and I'm trying to find him."

Henri pointed toward the man at the Faro table. "Go see Jack over there. The Professor spent a few hours in here night before last and he lost a lot of money to ole Jack. I'll bet he can tell you what you need. Although, why anyone would have to do with that deviltry is beyond me."

Henri crossed himself.

"Much obliged," Will said, then took his drink and walked to the Faro table.

As he approached, Jack looked up from his shuffling and gestured for Will to have a seat.

"Howdy," Will said.

"Greetings. Feeling lucky tonight, cowboy?" Jack said. He reached in the vest pocket of his silk vest, withdrew a silver flask and took a swallow.

"Just curious. I'm looking for Professor Uhrwerk. Mr. Lambert thought you might be able to tell me where he was headed."

Jack coughed and winced.

"Son, I'm a businessman. Tell you what. We talk while you play. Besides, you might win some in the process."

Will had seen folks play Faro, but he'd never felt he had the money to waste on it. It was easy enough. The cards are shuffled. You place your bet on a winning card lacquered to the tabletop. Three cards are dealt face up. The first card in the deck, called the "soda card", is discarded. The next card exposed is the losing card, and last is the winning card. If you put a marker on a king and a king shows up as the lose card, you lose your bet. If it shows up as the win card, you win even money. If a king shows up both times, you lose half your bet. There were other variations. You could bet for the given card to lose called "coppering", or bet for more than one card at time, but that was the gist of the game.

Will dug in his pocket and brought out a shiny $20 gold piece. He slid it across the table and laid his money on the Ace. "I heard Professor Uhrwerk played cards with you last night."

Jack smiled and shuffled the cards once more. Then he started dealing. "Yep, he was here and spent quite a bit of time with me. He's quite an interesting character, a man of high learning and low morals."

Jack discarded a four of diamonds, and then dealt a seven of spades to lose, and a Ten of Diamonds to win. The bet was still good. Jack looked to Will who shook his head and left his marker where it was.

"Do you know where the show was headed to? I would think that he would have gone toward the mining camps up north, or headed up to Denver. There ain't much else twixt here and California except Indian country," Will said.

"Again, the Professor is quite a character. He had a lot of questions, too. Wanted to know about some poison yellow rocks the Navajo call *leetso*. Worthless stuff, but he was powerful interested."

Jack smiled and dealt out the next pair of cards. "Now let's see what we have." He rolled a three of hearts to lose, and then an ace of clubs to win.

"There you go, son. Luck is on your side," Jack said slid a new $20 piece to Will.

"He was looking to find some rocks?"

Jack shrugged." I don't know. But I told him if here was interested in *leetso* that he should head out to the western part of the territory. Try again?"

Will considered it for a moment. "Do you know where exactly he was heading?"

Jack smiled. "I believe he did make mention of it."

THREE ACES FROM SATAN'S HAND

Will laid both $20 pieces on the Queen.

"A romantic, I see," the gambler said as he flipped the top card from the deck.

It was a Queen of Hearts to lose.

"Bit by the lady," Jack said. "Happens to all of us, son."

But there was one more card to go, there was still hope for another queen and Will would only lose one of the $20 pieces.

Jack dealt the final card. It was a Six of Spades.

"Sorry son, but that's Faro."

Jack took the two gold pieces from the board and slipped them into a pouch in his jacket pocket.

"Where did the Professor say he was headed?"

Jack took sip of his drink. "He was going to follow the old trail to Taos, then move on west toward the Shiprock. The Professor has got some crazy idea about trading to the Navajo for them yellow rocks. I think the old fellow is as crazy as a shithouse rat. But if you really want to find him, I believe he said that was setting up his medicine show tonight just outside town on the banks of French Lake. Just head along the road out of town and you won't miss it."

"You mean he's still in town?"

Jack smiled and raised his hands. "Ironic, isn't it? Care to play again?"

"I think I've done learned my lesson," Will said and stood up.

"If I were you, I'd consider it an investment in your education, young man."

Will started to walk away. But he stopped and turned back for a moment to ask one more question. "Did he have a girl with him?"

Jack smiled and looked up at Will. "Didn't that Queen of Hearts teach you nothing, boy?"

"Was there a girl?"

Jack shook his head. "No son. Far as I know the

Professor traveled alone."

"Much obliged, Mister," Will said and then began walking out of the saloon.

Jack called out after him. "Be careful, young man. There is something not right about that Professor Uhrwerk. And that damned horse of his is Lucifer's own."

Will mumbled a thank you, then went out, mounted up and headed along the trail toward French Lake.

❖

The medicine show was set up in a clearing close to the lake. Will saw that the festivities were already underway. A simple stage had been erected in front of the medicine wagon with the large painted side acting as a backdrop. Long boards had been placed over barrels for seating and about twenty people were in attendance. Horses and buckboards were left nearby.

The iron machine horse stood still like a guardian statue with only its eyes glowing red like a fading embers. It was left harnessed to the wagon and black braided ropes ran from the beast to bright lamps which shone upon the stage, illuminating it with a clean blue light that barely flickered.

There were no musicians to be seen, but the music from a hidden calliope filled the air. The Professor was working the crowd. He beat a tambourine in time with the music and encouraged the audience to clap along.

Will dismounted but did not approach. He stood leaning against Nell and watched from a distance just close enough to hear what was being said.

The song ended and the audience applauded heartily. Professor Uhrwerk raised his hands and went into his sales pitch." Uhrwerk's Uranium Tonic! *Damen und herren*, it is my firm belief that this is the one elixir that is capable of curing the many ills of mankind. It is capable of balancing the humors in a way in which no other tonic can hope to match. I have tested this elixir in a scientific study against *Herr* Bonnore's famous Electro Magnetic Bathing Fluid,

Townsend's Magic Oil, and various nostrums of the Kickapoo Indian Medicine Company and I can tell you that those other products are pure quackery. They have not one benefit in all of them and may in fact cause great harm to your health if used in excess.

"You may be saying that you feel fine. 'I'm as healthy as the horse,' you say. Well friends, let me ask you. Do you ever have trouble rising from bed in the morning? You eat well, you get plenty of rest, and yet it is not enough. You still hate to rise from that warm bed and begin your day of work. Do you ever feel that way, my friends? Well, it could well be the first sign of consumption. It may already be too late for you. Why wait? Why not infuse yourself with energy and life? If you feel poorly, why allow yourself to get worse? If you feel well, why not do something to feel better?

"Like it or not my dears, although you laugh and love now, seeds of death are even now growing within each and every one of you. Bit by bit, every single day, you are being dragged down into the grave. It is my sincere belief that secret electrical powers of the very universe are contained within uranium and my scientific experimentation has concocted this wondrous nostrum for the good of all mankind.

"My Uranium Tonic is good for gout, rheumatism, raging consumption, insidious catarrh, and a host of the feminine complaints. But I must tell you this one thing, my dears. I am afraid that I do not have enough tonic for any of you to purchase more than one bottle each. It contains exotic ingredients that are difficult and expensive to obtain. I only have a limited supply," he said and sadly shook his head.

"Although it pains me, not all of you can be helped. I must preserve a portion which I have promised to give to the needy."

The professor pulled on a brass stop on the side of the wagon and the music began again, this time a wild and vibrant tune. The eyes of the machine hours glowed red and the lamps began to flash. Professor Uhrwerk opened a wooden crate filled with bottles, grabbed a few and walked into the audience. He did a fine trade and each time he made a sale he spoke with the customer gravely and seriously as he passed the tonic to them, as if he were giving them the queen's crown jewels.

Finally, he had sold the entire case. He worked the brass stop again and the music ended. "I'm sorry my friends, but fear not. I will be back with more of this wondrous elixir. This is a time for a celebration of good health. You shall soon be hale and hearty and as full of energy as children. Allow me to close the evening's entertainment with a song from Cherie' the Nightingale of France."

Uhrwerk worked another stop and the wooded side of the wagon opened up, then Will saw what he had been waiting for. There she was, the girl from the dust storm. Just as lovely and fine as he had remembered her.

She wore a dress of white lace and she looked as delicate and fragile as a butterfly's wing. The sight of her took Will's breath away.

The crowd went silent as Cherie opened her perfect red lips and her voice rang out pure as the peal of a crystal bell into the night. Will didn't understand a word of it; the song was likely in French, he wasn't sure. But it was heart achingly beautiful.

At the end of her performance, she coyly bowed her head as the side of the wagon began to close. The crowd, including Will, burst into applause, standing and hooting and hollering in appreciation.

Just as she was hidden from view, Will clearly saw Cherie turn and look directly at him, and as before she gave him a secret wink with her gorgeous blue eyes.

The audience began to disburse. Will watched as a few customers came up to the professor. After some cajoling and the passing of additional money, they managed to talk

Uhrwerk into parting with more of the Uranium Tonic. Apparently the poor and unfortunate didn't need quite as much as the professor had originally figured on.

After a while, Professor Uhrwerk began to stare suspiciously at Will who still hadn't approached. "Can I help you, son?" he called out.

Will stepped closer. "I…uh….I was hoping that I might be able to have a word with Miss Cheri'."

A strange look game into Uhrwerk's eyes, then he laughed and shook his head. "*Nein doch*! No, my boy. I'm afraid that Cheri does not…see gentleman callers." He laughed again." Now, off with you. I have a lot to do."

Will flushed red and felt a rush of anger, but he reluctantly mounted up and rode away. Giving Nell a kick in the flanks so that he left at a gallop.

The more he thought about it the more he realized the situation that Cheri must be in. She was a virtual prisoner. It was up to him to do something about it, if she wanted him to, that is. He'd wait until Uhrwerk went to sleep, then sneak back and offer to take Cheri away.

What kind of life could she have in the back of a medicine wagon with that old fossil? Surely, she wanted to escape. If she did, he would rescue her and take her to the railhead at Trinidad or, if she had a hankering to, he wouldn't be adverse to taking her with him to California.

He still had a passel of money from the cattle drive. It was enough to start a life somewhere. And having a girl like Cheri would make it a fine one.

Several hours later, Will ambled back toward the medicine show encampment. Professor Uhrwerk had packed up most of the camp except for one tent. He watched the professor settle down for the night. Uhrwerk had moved some of the black braided ropes from the machine horse into the tent and strange lights flashed ominous shadows against the canvas walls for almost an hour. Finally, the lights dimmed and all was quiet.

Will crept into the camp and up to the back steps of the box wagon. What would Cheri do? Would she scream? He hoped he hadn't misinterpreted the wink she had given him.

"Cheri?" he whispered." Cheri?"

Will slowly parted the curtains and looked inside. The faint moonlight spilled inside and revealed Cheri's face. She turned and looked at him, smiling. She did not appear to be surprised at all. She was still fully dressed. It was as if she had been expecting him after all.

"My name's Will, ma'am. I know we ain't been rightly introduced."

Cheri said nothing.

"Oh, I reckon you don't speak much English." This was something he hadn't counted on. But in a way, it emboldened him.

"You probably won't understand any of this then, but I figure I'm gonna say it anyway. I know you don't know me. But I think you living like this is wrong. I'm more than willing to help you and get you out of here if you are of a mind to leave."

Cheri smiled and tilted her head toward the young cowboy, but still did not speak.

"I ain't got no family. Not since my brother James died in the war and my mama passed away. But I got a mind to go to California. You ain't gotta go with me if you don't care to. I'll take you anywhere you want to go, but I'd be mighty proud if you wanted to come with me to California, too.

"I ain't got much, but I'd share it all with you. Heck, you don't know what I'm saying, do you?"

Cheri did not answer, but she moved her delicate hand toward Will's cheek as if to caress it, but stopped before touching him.

Will looked toward her perfect face in the dim light." You are so beautiful. And that song, that was the prettiest thing I think I ever did hear."

Something seemed to change in Cheri. Her body shifted, and she drew back and suddenly began to sing. Not soft, but as loud as if she were in a concert hall.

Will jumped. "Cheri, hush up! What are you doing?"

But she continued her song. It was sad and haunting, nothing at all like the song she had sung in the medicine show.

Will heard rustling outside and then Uhrwerk's voice. "*Was is dieses leid?*"

There was no place to run. Uhrwerk was already out of his tent and it was too near the wagon to hope to escape. He moved farther into the wagon and tried to duck behind a box

Uhrwerk's face appeared. He held a gun in one hand and an object in his other hand that shot a bright light out before him. He spotted Will immediately.

"*Dieb! Dieb!*" he screamed as he brought up the revolver.

Will watched events unfold in slow motion. He knew in that instant that he was going to die and there wasn't anything he could do about it. He didn't even consider trying to draw his gun, Uhrwerk had the drop on him and he was going to die.

Just as the Professor fired, Cheri shot forward and placed herself in front of Will. Her side exploded from the blast.

"No!" Will screamed. His ears rang from the echo of the shot.

Cheri crumpled in a heap on the floor of the wagon. Uhrwerk seemed shocked by what he had just done and just stood there, struck dumb with the smoking gun hanging slack in his hand.

"*Unmöglich.* It is impossible."

Will moved toward Cheri. "You killed her you old bastard!"

"No. It is impossible. This could not have happened."

Will examined Cheri's wound and discovered not a drop of blood. In the illumination of Uhrwerk's light he saw beneath the tattered remnants of torn white lace not flesh, but an intricate maze of brass gears and wheels, some mangled and bent. A grating sound was coming from Cheri's throat instead of the bell like sound of her angelic voice. The inner wheels were ticking away more slowly with each passing second.

She was a broken clockwork machine. Her beautiful face really was made of porcelain. Her blue eyes were glass. There was no warmth in her body, only a cold metal framework of man made parts.

But still as Will looked in her artificial eyes, there seemed to be something more. "Cheri?" he whispered.

"She is only a machine, you foolish boy. She doesn't understand you."

The clicking within her body slowed and she turned her face toward Will.

"*Und* yet," Uhrwerk said, near to tears." I never made her to do anything like this….and that song, it was none I ever made her to sing."

Cheri smiled slightly, and just as her wheels stopped turning for the final time, she winked at Will with her sapphire eyes.

The End

CLAY ALLISON AND
THE HAUNTED HEAD

It was bad enough that the severed head was seeping blood through the burlap bag hanging from Clay Allison's saddle horn and onto his new boots, but when it started talking again, Allison was downright put out.

It all started three days previously in Elizabethtown, at Pearson's bar. Clay was sitting at a table playing poker with some locals when a Ute half-breed named Rosa came busting in. She was caterwauling and carrying on something fierce.

"Help me!" she screamed.

Clay had just been dealt a new hand and he took a quick peek at his cards. As he didn't have squat and was ahead on cash for the evening, he spoke up. "Men, I reckon we better end the game on this. There is obviously a female in distress."

Clay Allison was known as the Gentleman Gunfighter, but his gentle nature had a sight more to do with expediency than chivalry.

He stuffed his winnings into his pockets and tipped his hat to the other men at the table. Then he walked over to the distraught woman. "Calm down, Ma'am. How can I assist you?"

The men had all hell getting Rosa soothed enough to spit out her story, finally resorting to a double shot of rotgut whiskey to calm her nerves. This was not strictly legal as she was an Indian, but legality never took hold at Pearson's no how.

Rosa lived with Charles Kennedy on a small farm nearby in Palo Flechado Pass. They ran a traveler's rest to make hard currency between meager harvests. Her story of the goings on there was enough to chill the bones of even a strong man.

Everyone knew folks went missing sometimes. They fell down ravines, took sick betwixt here and there traveling on dangerous roads. They ran into wild Indians or desperadoes and come to a bad end. But lately, there had been more folks unaccounted than was usual.

Seems her Charlie was knocking his guests in the head and burying their bones in the root cellar. He made quite a profit on their possessions which they obviously no longer had use for. Then there was her mention of the contents of the smokehouse and what passed for jerky.

Tonight, Charles Kennedy exercised his predilection for homicide on their six year old son when the lad got a might too inquisitive and a might too mouthy about what he had discovered hidden in the smokehouse. To the horror of Rosa, the beast dashed the boy's brains out against the hearth. Then he locked her in the cabin and proceeded to drink himself into a stupor. She had only escaped by climbing out a narrow chimney to freedom.

Allison quickly formed a *posse*. When they busted down the cabin door Rosa's story was confirmed. The remains of the hapless boy were present as well as the bones of numerous travelers buried in shallow graves.

Kennedy was taken into custody and held in the local jail. The only question remaining in Clay Allison's mind was where the ill-gotten gains were hidden. Surely, there had been a fair portion of gold watches and silver somewhere to be claimed as evidence and held for "safe keeping." But the female was mute on the subject, confirming Allison's philosophy of never trusting a damn woman, much less an Indian.

Kennedy was arraigned a few days later on October 3, 1870 and the local magistrate was more than willing to hold him over until the District judge was able to travel to Elizabethtown for the trial. There was ample evidence. But the delay troubled the townsfolk. They were used to their justice being a bit swifter.

Rosa visited Allison that evening with concerns of her own.

"Senor Allison," she said. It was obvious she had been crying again. Those wet streaks across her cheeks were a permanent fixture at this point.

"Yes Ma'am? I hope you know I am busy."

Tonight Clay was in the hole financially and his hand had potential he didn't want the unlucky Ute woman to jinx. He was not inclined toward tolerance since he had neither received any of Kennedy's horde nor the dubious charms of the female, as any man would have assumed as his due for helping the last time.

"Senor, I must tell you. Charlie will not hang. He will get away."

Allison rolled his eyes. "We have a fine justice system. Although there have been times during which we have not seen eye to eye. I have no doubt he will get a fair trial and hang like the dog he is," he said then continued with the game. "I'll raise five dollars."

"But he will buy the judge. He has money, senor, much money."

Clay paused, considering, then lay his cards face down on the table and turned to look at Rosa. "We didn't find any treasure trove and you were mighty silent on the subject at the time."

"I was upset. I know he has the treasure." She bent to whisper in his ear. "I know where it is."

It was time to fold, in order to perform another errand of chivalry.

Allison rounded up another *posse* of townsmen, all righteous and true, to help dispatch a little prairie justice. Seems they could not, after all, trust the judge.

Allison, having seen his share of hangings, felt qualified enough to lead the good men to do the deed. They waited until the night guard retired to the outhouse, then they moved in quick and quiet.

Once inside, Allison and Stinky Johnson, faces masked by bandannas, grabbed the single cell's key from the desktop and crept to the door. Charles Kennedy lay sleeping on a cot in the corner, wrapped in a threadbare serape and oblivious to his surroundings.

Allison opened the door and he and his partner went to Kennedy and, in unison, tied the prisoner's hands and feet before he realized what was happening.

As the two men hefted him, Kennedy began to holler. "Help! Help! Who are you? Let me go!"

Stinky crammed a rag into Kennedy's mouth to silence his protests.

Allison and his helper ran as best as they could with the writhing form of Kennedy balanced between them. Other men helped to lift Kennedy over one of the horses and secured his body so it wouldn't slide off.

Allison and the rest of the posse mounted up and rode off, leaving a very confused deputy emerging from the outhouse, pants in one hand and a sheaf of penny dreadful pages in the other. On the far edge of Main Street, the men stopped and dismounted.

They threw Kennedy to the ground. He wallowed around some and managed to spit out his gag." I'm an innocent man! I never killed nobody! It's that lying woman you want! She's the cause of all of this," he said.

In spite of his protests, they looped a lariat around his neck. Allison tied the other end around his saddle horn and proceeded to spur his horse forward with a jolt, hurtling Kennedy around and dragging him forward. Allison made two galloping passes up and down the muddy main street of Elizabethtown. Each turn he made sent Kennedy's body tumbling like a rag doll on a string. So all assembled were amazed when, after Allison stopped, Kennedy struggled to rise. The man's clothes were ripped in a dozen places and caked with mud and horse shit and an angry red weal was visible along his neck.

He coughed and sputtered. "You don't understand. She's a witch. Please let me go." Kennedy's voice was gravelly from the damage done his throat by the cruel, rough rope.

Allison cursed and kicked his horse viciously causing the animal to jump and slam Kennedy forward by the neck into the dirt. Then Allison tore down Main Street one more time, galloping to beat hell with Kennedy jerkily following behind, his body bouncing across the hard dirt and crashing with crushing force against the hitching post in front of the General Mercantile.

Kennedy again wriggled to a sitting position. His face was covered with dirt and blood. He spit and sputtered and tried to speak.

"Oh hell" Allison said, still seated on his horse. He drew his pistol and took aim. "Just shut up and die." He let off a round and a neat hole appeared in the man's chest. "I hate to see a man grovel."

Kennedy fell backward. Everyone began to turn away and head home. The truth being that participating in a lynching was all good fun, but no one really wanted to be stuck with the job of clean up.

Then a gasp sounded from the remaining men as Kennedy spoke, this time his mouth filling with blood, making it that much more difficult to understand. "I can't die. She's got the magic. She done cursed me."

Clay Allison was perturbed. When he killed a man he expected him to stay dead. He dismounted with a disgusted grimace and drew the large Bowie knife from his belt. "That's enough, by God. This is ending now."

He took Kennedy by the hair and whipped the Bowie knife down with wicked force, once, twice, three times and then stood with the severed head aloft. The headless body fell back again, but this time, aside from a few random jerks, it stayed where it fell.

Allison raised the head to stare at Kennedy face to face. "You look dead enough to me, ha, ha," he said and looked at the men around him. Two of them were vomiting and the rest looked blanched white as ghosts.

"Come on now, that's funny. He had it coming. You saw what he did to that boy."

If they disagreed they didn't speak. It wasn't wise to argue with Clay Allison as too many men had already discovered. He was unpredictable and the graveyard always had room for one more. They just slowly walked away as Allison wiped the bloody blade on the clothing of the dead man.

That Rosa woman had done another vanishing act. Understandable, he supposed, but she had been too damnably vague on the location of the Kennedy's collected loot. Still, the evening had turned out to be entertaining enough. He'd track her down later and make her give up the location of the treasure. He'd be damned if she would deny him that prize again.

"Stinky, fetch a buckboard and take this dead dog to the dump at the end of town."

"What about that?" Stinky asked, pointing at the head.

"Oh, I got plans for this," said Allison.

Allison took a burlap sack out of his saddlebag, stuffed the head inside then tied it to the saddle horn. He didn't feel remorseful about tonight's grim work. In fact, he felt like celebrating. He'd go see the Frenchman at Lambert's Saloon and have a few drinks. If he was lucky, the Frenchman would have some dinner left.

Henri Lambert (or *On-ray Lam-bear* as he kept telling folks) used to be a personal chef to General Grant and to that bastard Lincoln. Allison didn't much care for the former employers, but the Frenchman was a damn good cook.

He'd mount the killer's head on a spike outside the saloon. It would bring in business and serve to warn all that wanton lawlessness wouldn't be tolerated. Better yet, the Frenchman could charge a nickel to see it and give Clay a cut.

As he mounted his horse and turned toward Lambert's, he heard a muffled sound coming from the burlap sack. Or at least it had seemed to come from the sack. Allowing his horse to continue its slow walk toward the end of town, Allison untied the top of the sack and looked in.

Charles Kennedy's face, covered with fresh blood, looked up at him from the bottom of the sack. Its eyes were open and sharp. "Why the hell did you have to do that?"

Clay Allison had seen a lot of things. He had been a spy for the Confederacy and seen things no man should be forced to see. He had been captured behind enemy lines and taken prisoner, doomed to hang. But he had escaped the hellhole they called a prisoner of war camp. He had seen many horrors, but never had a dead man spoken to him.

"What in hell?"

"Look at me! I have eternal life as a head in a sack."

"You talk?" Clay asked.

"So do you, but you don't listen for shit. I kept trying to tell you Rosa is a damned witch."

"I still don't believe you. This is just proof you are in league with the devil himself."

"Why lie now? I've got nothing to lose. I'm nothing but a trophy head and she is still out causing mischief."

Clay smiled.

"What are you doing?" Charlie's head asked.

"Henri is gonna shit when he sees you." With that, Clay tied the bag shut again, muffling the protests of the head. A nickel? Hell, they could charge a dollar!

Clay dismounted and tied up his horse at the hitching post in front of Lambert's Saloon. Then, taking the burlap bag with him, he swaggered inside.

The oil lamps were shining brightly and the music from the piano filled the room with jovial warmth. But when the clientele caught a glance of Clay Allison and his bloody burden the mood immediately took on a more somber tone.

Clay smiled and approached the bar. Several men vacated to clear a spot for the gunfighter.

Henri Lambert looked at Allison and shook his head disapprovingly.

"Henri, I would like two shots of whiskey. One for me and one for Charlie here." He reached into the sack, grabbed a handful of hair and placed the head on the bar in front of him.

Henri grimaced." Oh no! Mr. Allison, please take that thing away. You will upset all my customers."

"Really? Well, what do you think, Charlie?" Allison turned to the head.

Charles Kennedy's head did not respond. In fact, it sat there glassy eyed and oozing on Henri's counter top like so much rotting meat in the New Mexico night. A fly buzzed in and landed on its nose.

Clay drew his pistol. "Talk you son of a bitch," he said then cocked back the hammer and put the barrel between the eyes of the severed head.

"Please Mr. Allison! Think of the mess it would make."

A man behind Allison began to laugh. Clay narrowed his eyes and turned. A miner dressed in mud-stained clothes sat nearby, giggling hysterically and slapping his knee.

"That's a good one for sure, Mr. Allison. That's the funniest thing you done since you danced naked on the bar with the red ribbon on your pecker." The man was practically in tears he was laughing so hard.

Clay Allison was not laughing, he wasn't even smiling: a fact that appeared to slowly dawn on the miner.

"You calling me a liar?" Clay said, his words icy and clear. "You saying this head don't talk?"

The man paled. "No, Clay — Mr. Allison, Sir, that ain't what I meant at all. I just—"

"No man calls me a liar and walks away. That's an insult to my honor, and I aim to get satisfaction."

The other customers began to clear that end of the room. Henri muttered a few curses in French, grabbed some of the more expensive bottles from the bar and also moved to a safe distance.

The man raised his hands in the air. "Mr. Allison, I meant no disrespect, Sir. I'm sorry I—"

"Everybody heard this man say I was lying. Now I'm calling him out, fair and square." Clay waved the gun around the room, but kept his stern eyes on the petrified miner.

Allison made a big pantomime show of holstering his pistol, then he glanced back at Henri and the rest of the cringing crowd.

At that instant, the miner rose from his chair and made a break for the front door. Allison drew fast as the hand of God and shot the man in the back.

Allison looked at the crowd, steely eyed. "You saw him. He was trying to get the drop on me."

Heads nodded in quick succession, a single voice said "Y -y-yes sir, Mr. Allison, it was surely self-defense."

"Damn right!" Allison preened. "Now, anybody else want to say this here head don't talk?"

"No, no," came the nervous mutter of the crowd, along with "Lord save us" and one brave soul in the rear piped in "I can hear it now. Is that 'Camptown Races' it's a'singin'? "

Luckily this smoothed Allison's feathers for he turned to Henri, tipped back the last of his drink, followed by

Charlie's, then shoved the head roughly back into the burlap sack. He stalked out of the saloon making sure to knock the sides of the sack against each chair and flinching customer as he passed.

Henri could hardly wait until Allison swept grandly out the door to heave a sigh of relief. He mopped down the bar with clean, soapy water, paying special attention to the spot where the head had sat.

Allison tossed the sack roughly over the saddle horn.

"Ow!" cried Charlie's head, "Whadya go and do that for?"

"That was for making me look the fool in front of Henri and half the town. I have a mind to dump your sorry head in the nearest latrine! Why didn't you talk in there? We could'a made some good money," said Allison.

"I'm a little shy in front of large groups. Besides, only special people can hear me—people who might just make a whole lot more money by doin' a man a favor instead of sellin' looks at a talking head for a nickel apiece. You're a special man Allison, and even though it were you and your posse what did me in, I'll tell you where all my money and gold is stashed. All you gotta do is take me to where my body is. You owe me at least that," said Charlie's head.

"I don't believe I owe you a thing, you murderous man-eating dog. But as I am a compassionate fellow and believe if a man is to go to his eternal rest he should do it with all his pieces in the same place. I'll help you to reunite with your body. And I'll take the gold too, seeing as how I'm going to be doing all of your walking for you."

The body wasn't at the dump where he directed Kennedy's body to be taken. From the looks of things, blood, drag marks and other signs, it had been there and then taken away again by person's unknown. Some damned goody-two-shoes, no doubt.

Allison was getting a mite irritated, and was feeling a bit peculiar as he rode and not just the regular peculiar one might feel when following the directions of an ill-natured, foul tempered, severed head. This was more the feeling one got when sensing something just outside his line of sight and too quiet to recognize. Misty moving visions, shadows on the periphery and veiled whispers were carried on the breeze. There were some mighty powerful spiritual forces at work he didn't understand. But he did understand the power of gold. And, one way or another, this head in a gunny sack was gonna give up the loot.

He pulled up alongside the ruts made by Kennedy's body being dragged away.

"All right, Charlie, what's this all about?" Allison peered into the sack.

"How the Hell should I know? I've been here with you the whole time. Unless. . . yes! Rosa! I told you she was a witch! I bet she done dragged off my body to use in one of her spells," said Kennedy.

"You'd best have some way of finding out where your body is and how close we are to it. I'm getting a mite perturbed and would just as soon leave you to the coyotes and go have myself a drink than spend any more time wandering around in the dark like a damned 'possum," said Allison.

"I only have a vague sense. I think it might be this way," said Kennedy as he jiggled in the sack toward the south." Yes, I can feel it. But hurry, I got a bad feeling she is doing something evil."

Allison sighed in disgust and spurred his horse onward. He'd ridden about an hour and had about convinced himself it was folly, when something changed in the air. At about half a mile towards a dense tree line, it seemed the whispering in his mind was growing louder and the hair on his neck beginning to rise. Perhaps it was the same strange force drawing Kennedy.

"We're almost there," said the severed head.

The whispers grew and more shadows darted crazily just out of sight. No matter how fast Clay turned his head, he always missed what it was. His horse began to spook.

It began crow hopping from side to side and finally stopping, refusing to go any further. He dismounted and took the sack, hefted it over his shoulder like Saint Nicholas and kept walking south. Kennedy's head began to jiggle excitedly.

"All right, Head," Allison said. "It looks like we've got to hoof it from here. Let me remind you again, if you're somehow leading me on like a fool I will make you very sorry you were ever born. Or spawned. Or however devils like you come to be."

"You mean you haven't already? Ow!" yelled Kennedy as Allison 'accidentally' switched shoulders to carry him and bumped the head against a particularly rough tree trunk. Moaning, he continued, "All right. I understand."

The wind picked up, swirling eddies in the dust around Allison's boots. For the first time in his life, Allison seriously considered he might be dealing with spirits not of an alcoholic nature. And speaking of, he sure could use a good stiff drink right about then. As soon as this was over, he would walk into Henri's and drink until he ran out of money or passed out.

The wind picked up and the night became even darker. Allison came over a ridge and stood at the top of the rise looking down on a circular clearing surrounded by small trees. In the center was freshly dug earth with a suspiciously large man-shaped lump.

"It's here! It's here!" Kennedy's head bucked and wiggled in the sack, which suddenly caused it to split. The head hit the ground with a thud. The head began to drag along with a side-winding motion using its tongue and natural momentum to roll.

Allison gaped at Kennedy's hasty departure." See here, you ornery cuss! Don't you try to get out of showing me where your treasure is hid!"

The head entered the circle of scrub brush and the greenery burst into flame like torches made by Mother Nature herself. Allison flinched and nearly wet himself, something he hadn't done while sober since he was a tiny lad.

"Here, Clay! Dig here. Hurry if you want the treasure!" Kennedy rasped, his tongue coated with drying dirt.

As Clay walked into the circle, a dark swarm descended, as if a defensive cloud of flies. The blackness raced around the circle, round and past Allison, almost seemed to try to push him away from the treasure. He dropped to his knees and began to dig in the loose soil with his hands.

Allison found a gold nugget the size of an aggie marble. Then a cold hand emerged from the dirt and snapped tight on Allison's throat and stopped him in mid-shriek. He toppled backward, trying to get away. This succeeded in pulling the rest of Kennedy's deceased yet animated corpse out of the ground.

The black swarm descended nearby. The buzzing quieted and the mass coalesced into a figure. It was Rosa, Kennedy's half-Ute wife, she of the tear stained cheeks and the undying but never displayed gratitude.

"I told you she was a witch!" screamed Kennedy's head.

"At least I am not a demon who kills for sport. A demon who kills for gold. A demon who devours its own young!" spat Rosa.

"Well, let me tell you, Mr. Allison," said Kennedy as his body grasped his head from the ground and put it back in its proper place. As the severed parts touched, an unholy light fused them together." The boy tasted the best."

Kennedy stood up and stretched his battered body, twisting the flesh to change into a new shape of his own, a horrible amalgam of man and demon, lizard and snake. His evil smile widened, splitting the frail human skin of the cheeks as the outgrowing rows of jagged teeth stretched back, impossibly, to nearly the back of his head. He leaned in close to Allison and whispered in his ear on fetid breath "Yesss. . . the boy tasted best!"

Clay wet himself, but he never admitted it to any man.

"*Senor*!" Rosa yelled wildly, vying for Allison's attention with his shock. "The blood of the victims cries out for vengeance. Use their power!" Rosa shouted. "We can kill him but you have to get the gold! "

Allison, being fond of his hide, snapped out of his daze. He looked at the gold nugget which began to melt in his hand, like warm butter, changing from shiny gold to blood red in color. As much as he hated giving it up, Allison saw no other choice. He threw the bloody nugget at Kennedy and began to scrabble around for more and more. Each time he found something, a nugget, coin or watch, it changed in his hands from gold to blood.

Each object stuck to Kennedy like tar, then ran over its skin like a living thing. Kennedy began to scream and tried to remove the red substance like he'd been splashed with Hellfire itself. Allison kept digging, scrambling for all he could find. Finally he threw the last of it, a silver framed picture of a little girl. This struck the demon squarely in the face, the frame became a melted blood colored patch, forming a seal over the slitted eyes and terrible mouth.

The thing which called itself Charlie Kennedy fell and lay rolling on the ground in agony.

Rosa turned to Allison. "You are almost as bad as him. But leave the circle now and you may survive a while longer. Leave now!"

Allison quickly complied, falling over himself as he rushed away. Rosa, staying within the inner ring proceeded to spread something from a sack which looked like rock salt all around the outer edge. She stood next to Kennedy's struggling, prone form. "I must make this right," she said softly.

The night darkened suddenly as the flaming brush began to burn a cold black fire. This blinded Allison momentarily as he tried to focus on what was happening before him. Moaning came from inside the circle. The demon Kennedy cursed Rosa as best as it could and Rosa chanted back at the demon in what sounded like her own native Ute at first, then languages unrecognized by Allison. The bloody gold covering the demon's body began to pulsate.

"Justice!" Rosa screamed at Kennedy. "The spirits are having their revenge. You spilled their blood for their gold, it is fitting."

Allison watched as she took more of the substance from the bag and began to pour it over the demon. The bloody gold faded along with the flesh of the demon. The corpse began to whither until there was nothing left but a dried husk, a paper thin skin like a dead locust wing.

Rosa was soon surrounded by ghostly forms, more than Allison could count. She took a second sack out of her pocket and scattered what looked like yellow cornmeal around and tossed it into the air. The spirits glided through the meal, dove and flitted like happy birds on a fine spring day.

"Go in peace," she said.

Allison stared as the spirits fluttered then winked out until only one remained, a small boy. The boy smiled at Rosa, sad and sweet. The flames turned red and warm and fought back the chill night and the darkness.

Rosa called out "Senor Allison. Go now—don't look back."

Allison walked towards the edge of the clearing where his horse waited, but he could not help but watch as Rosa went to her son. She took out one last thing from her pocket, a small bottle. She doused herself with the contents and walked into the fire and burst into flame.

Rosa, engulfed in flame, danced on the demon's husk corpse, measured steps as she sang softly. She kicked and danced and the dry mummified corpse became an inferno. She kicked the ashes and cinders to scatter in the wind and vanish like fireflies. She seemed to feel no pain. On the contrary, it seemed a joyful dance. When the corpse was nothing but a memory, her spirit son came into her arms and they embraced, flying apart in cinders and floating into the night sky.

Allison was stunned, yet exhilarated. They would say he was a madman back in Elizabethtown if he told the story of what had occurred this night.

He caught up with his horse and pulled the emergency bottle of whiskey from his saddlebag. He took a long swallow, then mounted and turned north toward Lambert's saloon. Before he was halfway there he began stripping off his clothes.

"Camptown ladies sing this dis song, doo-dah, doo-dah," he sang, and then Allison screamed at the moon hanging over the hills of Cimarron. "Call me a liar, you sons of bitches! But you had better be ready to die!"

The End

AFTERWORD

Believe it or not, most of this story is true.

A couple of years back, we decided to stop for a spell during a 3,000 mile motorcycle run at a place called the St. James Hotel in Cimarron, New Mexico.

I ordered a much needed beer at the saloon and asked the barkeep about the history of the place. He related the story of Clay Allison's act of decapitation along with several other ghostly tales of the area.

Now, whether than head talked or not is a matter of conjecture, or maybe a matter of how many beers you had occasion to consume.

But the bloody events of that night are still talked about to this day. Being the opportunistic writer I am, I figured I would team up with the lovely and talented Sherri

Dean to tell the tale in our own way.—*Bill D. Allen*

Bill and I share many things—beer, a love of spooky things, and a brain. Granted, not everyone shares well, but we have it down to a science—mad science that is.

When he told me the gentleman gunslinger story tale, the enthusiasm rolled out of me and didn't stop until the end of the story you see before you.

Keep your salt handy!—*Sherri Dean*

ANNIE OAKLEY AND THE TERROR OF THE WORLD'S FAIR

It began the evening I overheard bickering from Mr. Cody's tent. My husband Frank and I had just returned from an evening touring the exposition. We particularly enjoyed the presentation by Nicola Tesla at the Westinghouse Electricity Hall, the amazing uranium electric automatons of Doctor Hermann Uhrwerk, and model of the mighty cannon currently being built by Carnegie steel which is to send daring adventurers through the aether to land on the moon five years hence.

I enjoyed the speech by Susan B. Anthony, although I fear my poor Frank was scandalized. I explained to him that once Dr. Uhrwerk's automatons took over all the housework, we women were going to have to occupy ourselves and he had might as well get used to it.

We had taken a carriage back to the fifteen acre grounds between 62nd and 63rd street, adjacent to the Midway Plaisance where Buffalo Bill's Wild West and Congress of the Rough Riders of the World had set up shop. The eighteen thousand seat arena and associated vendor booths, souvenir shops and scores of tents for the performers were as neatly arranged as a strict military encampment in contrast to the chaotic haphazard arrangements of the Midway just next door. The great Chicago Ferris wheel loomed over the entire grounds like a celestial relic from Apollo's chariot. The glow from the exposition's magical electric lights, powered by Mr. Tesla's noisy generators warmed the night.

I left my dear husband Frank at my quarters to ready himself for bed, and walked to Mr. Cody's tent to discuss final preparations for tomorrow's show. I stopped short at the sound of a tumultuous argument. I must confess that I did eavesdrop, but did so with the best of intention, as you will see. I kept to the shadows and peered into the illuminated confines of Cody's quarters through the parted door flap.

Cody stood leaning over his desk, pointing at the man's chest with a deerskin gloved finger. "I not going to cough up one plug nickel, Mr. Coughlin. That idiot Mr. Wacker and his bunch of church hens and college professors didn't want our show because we were too rough and tumble, a circus of unsophisticated louts and savages. Buffalo Bill's Wild West was too course for your fine White City. Well, it's too late now. You have killed the golden goose and I'll be damned if I let you bully your way in now."

Coughlin took a puff of his cigar. "You, Sir, are profiting from the notoriety and draw of the exposition and an honorable man would realize that he needs to pay his fair share to those he is leeching off of," Coughlin said. "The City of Chicago is footing quite a bill to ensure proper police protection, sanitation and the like."

Coughlin was a bull of a man. His broad shoulders and beer barrel midsection strained the confines of his starched white shirt and fancy suit coat. The collar was tight around his thick neck. His beet red cheeks and chin were shaved clean leaving no sideburns which accentuated the prominent black mustache he sported bat wings from his upper lip. He looked like he was fixing to explode any minute like a cheap balloon between the heat of Cody's tent and the subject of their conversation.

"An honorable man, Mr. Coughlin wouldn't try to change the game when he started to lose. I made them a fair offer at the time and was turned down. So, I thumbed by nose at them and set up the show across right across from the midway. It's not my fault they the lacked good sense and vision as to what the American public wants to purchase. Besides, since my show started a month before yours, perhaps your 'World Exposition', and all you crooked Chicago aldermen owe me a royalty for bringing all this business to *you*."

"You may be a big man out West Cody, but in Chicago, nobody crosses Bathhouse Coughlin. You keep that in mind."

"A braggart is a braggart from here to Timbuktu. I don't cotton to them and I don't suffer fools. You take your starched monkey suit and your ten cent cigar and all your Irish louts and get out of here pronto."

The man took a big puff and let it out in Cody's face. "Accidents happen," he said. "People get hurt."

I took that moment to enter the room and I extracted a pistol from my handbag.

Coughlin stiffened at the unmistakable sound of the hammer cocked. "That they do, Sir," I said.

Coughlin slowly turned and faced me, his eyes insolently passing up and down my form. "I assume you are the famous Annie Oakley."

"Assume what you will sir, I would however request that you direct your attention to the Smith & Wesson Model 3 pointed between your eyes. I would suggest that this would be an opportune time for you to leave."

Coughlin appeared to almost spit out a retort, but thought better of it. Looked back at Cody, then at me with contempt in his eyes and then stormed out of the tent. At the door flap be paused and pointed back at Mr. Cody with his cigar and began to utter some vile comment.

The words died in his throat as a shot rang out and his cigar disintegrated in his hand.

"Whoops, dear me. Accidents indeed," I said cocking the pistol again. "I seem to be so clumsy today."

Coughlin, a shade whiter that he had been seconds before, exited quickly and quietly.

I returned my pistol to its hiding place in my handbag. "All right Bill, who, pray tell, was that beastly man?"

"Bathhouse Coughlin, come to shake us down for protection money."

"Oh? And from what does he suppose we need protection?"

"His thugs. That ruckus we had last night was a band of his Irish hooligans. Our rough riders made quick work of them. Send them riding home wearing bonnets and tied on the backs of donkeys. That sort of thing might work on gentile city folk, but he'll have a difficult time flustering our compound with a few big talking buffoons. Don't trouble yourself with it, Ma'am."

I quickly completed my business with Mr. Cody. Although he was dismissive of the threat and full of bravado, it turned out that Bathhouse Coughlin was good on his word.

It was a week later when the first death occurred. One of the Cossacks didn't show up for the show. The rest of the troop were able to get through the act and when the marksman Johnny Baker took the center of the arena his compatriots went looking. They found his broken body behind the Indian village. None knew what to make of the death.

Suspicion, as usual, was placed on the Comanches, the Sioux and the other Indian tribes who shared their encampment. No matter how Mr. Cody insisted that they be treated with respect if there was ever a missing saddle blanket, bottle of fire water or gold watch, the white performers always put blame on the Indian band. But there was no way to prove anything and the death of the young Ukrainian remained a mystery. It received some small coverage in the Daily Tribune, but it wasn't unusual, as the brute had said "accidents happen."

There was a small memorial service held the next day just before the afternoon show. A large flower arrangement was delivered anonymously. After the service Mr. Cody gestured at Frank and me. He looked grave and had a piece of paper in his hand.

"Bill, what's wrong?" Frank asked.

Cody sighed. "I feel that I have a duty to warn you. This letter came with that monstrous flower delivery. It isn't signed, but I think we can be sure it came from our friend Coughlin. It reads: *Too bad about the trick rider, good thing it wasn't one of your headliners. It would be awful if something happened to them. Be very careful. It is a dangerous world we live in.*"

"Do you think Annie is in danger?" Frank said.

"I think we should take precautions just in case," Cody answered.

"Gentleman, you should know me well enough by now to realize that I can take care of myself," I said. Gallant as it was, I have never been some delicate orchid requiring constant care and attention.

"Of course, but this man is capable of anything. We will redouble our efforts to make sure that no unauthorized persons are allowed in the housing areas after hours. It is only sensible to take precautions," Mr. Cody said.

The show must go on, and it did of course. The bandstand of the horseshow shaped arena was filled to capacity. It was a fine day and we all took our positions for the opening ceremonies. William Sweeny's cowboy band played the Star Spangled Banner and we took off our hats and covered our hearts as one. The color guard displayed the grand flag with the forty-four stars flying in the light breeze.

The Grand Review began. Each contingent of riders

paraded around the arena in full regalia. The Cossacks from the Ukraine, the Syrian and Arabian horsemen, the Mexican vaqueros, the military contingents of the 6th U.S. Calvary, the "Potsdammer Reds" of German King William II, the French Cuirassiers, a British company of 12th Lancers from Wales, and the wild Cossacks.

The Indian tribes followed, some of the crowd booed as usual, some throwing apple cores and other waste items even though it was expressly forbidden. It was all pageant and pomp and spectacle, and after you had seen it hundreds of time it was simply boring. My show was next and my thoughts were on preparation.

Frank assisted me and we astonished the crowd of onlookers. Truth be told my rifle shots were made with bird loads for the show, but I had been hunting squirrels since I was eight years old and although it was not virtuous to be prideful I have always been a crack shot. Frank knew it, or he would never let me shoot a lit cigarette from his lips. This also kept some civility in our martial condition. It would be foolish to upset a woman who made her income shooting things.

I took my bows after the show as they set up for the horse race which followed. I was determined not to let Coughlin or any other living soul make me live in fear. Although I was born lowly Phoebe Ann Moses I had created myself to be Annie Oakley and Annie was a hard woman.

The scream in the night was horrific. It was a shrill, agonizing cry that tore through my breast into my core. I grabbed my pistol, threw open my tent flap and rushed into the night.

"Annie! Wait!" Frank called and rushed to follow.

I saw the poor boy lying on the ground forty feet from my tent. It was the young Arab who had just brought me my dinner tray. His white robes were soaked with blood and soiled with the filth of the muddy ground. So small, so broken. He looked like a discarded doll. So still and obviously lifeless.

Frank rushed behind me. He held a Winchester rifle. "Are you mad? You can't risk yourself like that...." Then he saw the child. "Oh my God. How dreadful."

Others came, among them Bill Cody. "Get back, let me see to him," he said.

Cody knelt next to the boy, carefully examining his wounds and the surrounding muddy ground. Frank and I approached cautiously. "What do you think happened?" I asked.

"He's been trampled to death. Likely that's what happened to the Cossack as well, but it wasn't so obvious when the ground was dry. Do you see these hoof prints?" He indicated the confusion of marks everywhere, deeply impressed in the ground.

"Yes, what was it?"

"A Buffalo."

"A buffalo did this? Where is it now?" I said.

He looked down the alleyway between tents. "The tracks lead that way."

He rose, and Frank and I followed, weapons at ready. We followed the retreating prints through the muddy alleyway. They continued fifty feet or so then they ended, or changed rather—into the bare footprints of a human being.

A cold chill ran down my back and an icy hand clutched at my heart. This was unnatural, evil, and I had an idea of what it was.

"But," Cody said. "I don't understand."

"I do, Bill. I've read tales from the dark hills of Europe. This is a type of monster the peasants feared in the dark of the full moon. A lycanthrope."

"But, isn't that a wolf?" Cody asked.

"I hardly see the difference, it's a beast man," I said. "Besides, which is more powerful? In all your experience, have you ever seen a lone wolf take down a healthy, adult bison? Perhaps the beast has simply chosen a more powerful form, one more closely identified with you."

"So, he found a way to harm us after all," Cody said.

"But that poor boy, why would they kill him?" I asked. "What does it prove? How cruel they are? The show will go on despite this tragedy."

Cody nodded. "He wasn't after the boy. He was trying to kill you. The boy had just left your tent. In the darkness, it would have been difficult to tell the difference between this poor boy in those robes and your small frame. This could have been you, Annie. They want us shut down and they are willing to kill using the Devil's own black arts to do it."

A cold child rushed through me and I drew back, stepping into a figure who had quietly walked up behind me. I screamed and turned around to see a buffalo robe wrapped figure holding a piece of jerky.

"*Watanya Cicilla,*" he said smiling, "Sorry for scaring you."

"Chief Sitting Bull," I answered, trying to calm myself. "What brings you to this side of the camp, and so late? I do hope we haven't disturbed your rest." Although time was wearing down the great chieftain, he was still a proud warrior of the Plains at heart.

"I would have to be deaf to sleep through this noise. Besides, I wanted a snack. What goes on here?" he said then took a bite from the jerky, chewing noisily.

I glanced toward Bill who made a motion with his chin back toward the alley. I perceived that he wished me to take the chief away from the grisly scene. I smiled and took the Chief's arm, guiding him gently back down the alleyway.

Sitting Bull had joined the Wild West show after years of cajoling by Bill himself, but not because of it. He agreed to join only after seeing my sharp shooting performance and meeting me in person afterward. He told me that he saw me as a kindred spirit to his daughter, a proud Indian maiden who perished at the Battle of Big Horn and was forever lost to him. He had adopted me, in his own way, calling me "*Watanya Cicilla*" which meant "Little Sure Shot" in his Lakota tongue.

"I hear other things too," he said "Things carried on the wind that say evil comes. There are spirits, talking, bringing trouble. The spirits talk of you, dear one, and I worry for you."

He gently touched my cheek with a single fingertip, a gesture that would have incited rage among the average populace that still feared the "wild red savages," but I was not afraid. To the contrary, it was as if he had placed a magic mark of protection upon me to guard me from the evil he feared was coming. I was more than willing to accept any blessing the old chief would bestow. She was so happy that he had stayed with the show rather than return to the Standing Rock Reservation. She had feared for his life there as the Indian Agents were known for their abuse of power.

"Thank you for your concern, Chief. Mr. Cody has everything under control for now."

"What happened to that boy?" Sitting Bull asked.

"Trampled by a horse," Cody interjected. He had left the side of the corpse and walked over to join us. "A horrible tragedy, but nothing to worry yourself about. You should go back to your tent and rest. I worry that you push yourself too hard."

The great chief looked back over my shoulder. "Horse, eh? Ha! Okay, Cody you are the big hunter. I will go back to bed."

He turned to me and raised a finger. "*Watanya Cicilla*. As my daughter once was, you are a strong headed woman who can protect herself."

He made a sly grin. "But remember that everyone needs help now and again."

He dropped his raised hand and clutched his battered buffalo robe a little tighter around his shoulders and padded softly away into the darkness of the camp. I watched him go, an ill feeling of spirit in my gut, until he disappeared into the night.

Mr. Cody was adamant that the Indians were not to be told of details of the incident, but were instead informed that the boy had wandered in amongst the horses and been trampled accidently. It was plausible enough, it you weren't familiar with how knowledgeable and competent the Arabs, even the young ones, were around the stock. I have no knowledge as to how Cody and his partner Mr. Salsbury made restitution to the poor boy's father in order to avoid a calamitous revolt amongst the Arabs and Syrians. But for the moment things were calm.

Cody had expressed the belief that if the over one-hundred-sixty Indians had gotten wind of this beast creature that they would all have abandoned the show out of superstitious fear, leaving them with an insurmountable difficulty. He was determined that we handle the problem ourselves.

I do believe that he felt a bit of his youthful spirit in this quest. Bill Cody considered himself a mighty hunter and never before had he had such potential prey. He asked me to investigate the legends further and provide him with a weapon with which to slay the creature

The next day Frank accompanied me to the Chicago Public Library, but learned little. I did discover that the term lycanthrope came from the Greek myth of the curse of King Lycaon. In one version of the tale, Zeus cursed the bloodthirsty ruler and all his kin by turning them into wolves after they killed Arcas, one of Zeus's many sons from his liaisons with mortal woman. But alas, nothing of worth came of it. There was not a single reference to how one might slay such a beast.

We returned to the fairgrounds and sought the counsel of Mr. Frederick Jackson Turner, the professor who lectured on the American West with our troupe. He was a man of letters and I prayed that he might have some knowledge as to such folklore.

Again our hopes were dashed. He had no expertise in the subject matter whatsoever and considered such superstition beneath contempt. However, he suggested that if we were truly interested in delving into such tripe that we might have some luck with the spiritualists and *fakirs* on the Midway. In particular, there was one young man who had the reputation of studying such supernatural nonsense.

He wrote down the name and handed it to Frank who read it aloud." Erik Weisz?"

I stifled chuckle.

"You know him?" Frank asked.

"Oh yes, I know the young man. Although he is better known as Harry Houdini."

I'd met Mr. Weisz when he'd come to speak with me after I had finished my afternoon show a while back. He was fascinated with my sharpshooting. Considering himself a master illusionist, I soon came to realize that he suspected my ability somehow had more to do with illusion than skill and seemed determine to discover how I was able to accomplish my tricks.

I gave the young man a private shooting exhibition and chose to let my shooting reflect the truth of the matter. Initially I was a bit put out, being questioned by such an arrogant young man, but soon I realized that he was passionately seeking truth, not attempting to label me a fraud. He left convinced I was indeed as skilled as purported to be and we were mutually respectful of each other. His boyish charm and earnest manner were delightful and I was more than happy to visit the young man to see if he could aid us.

Frank and I pedaled our bicycle built for two over to visit Mr. Weisz at his booth on the Midway. When we arrived he and his brother, a lad named nicknamed Dash were taking a break between shows. They tossed an old baseball back and forth out in front of their large "Amazing Houdini Brothers" sign while Erik rehearsed his patter for the next show. When they spotted Frank and me they stopped and came to greet us, Erik offering to help me off the bike, although I really didn't need it.

"My dear Mrs. Oakley! Best sharpshooter in the land!" he proclaimed and bowed with a flourish. He took my hand and kissed it lightly, which I allowed as it was all in good fun. He looked to Frank as he did so, and Frank gave him a sour scowl.

"You grace me with your presence dear lady!" Erik said. "Whatever may I do for you on this fine afternoon? Dash!" he called to his brother. "Fetch the wondrous Miss Oakley a seat, you cad! We mustn't have her fainting from fatigue!"

Dash, smiling, ran off to fetch a chair for me.

He returned in a moment. He'd managed to locate one for Frank as well, inviting us to sit. "My apologies, dear folk," he said, "but I cannot stay to converse. I will leave you to my brother as I'm bound for a most educational exhibition of Algerian Dancers from Morocco."

I smiled." I believe most of the folk on the Midway refer to that particular educational exhibition as Little Egypt's hoochie coo show."

Dashed turned somewhat red, smiled and raised his hands in defeat." Alas, I must confess that she also plays some small part in the production. Still, we have been so busy with our act that I haven't been able to attend the spectacle prior to today. I hope you will pardon me."

I smiled and nodded." Of course, good sir."

With that he donned he tipped his hat courteously and left us three to talk.

"Mr. Weisz, I'm afraid I've come in regard to a serious matter. We have need of your expertise regarding the supernatural. You come highly recommended."

He smiled and rolled his eyes with fake modesty. "Pish-posh, me? Of course I shall help with whatever knowledge I possess."

Given his propensity for the study of all things magical I should not have been surprised to find him such a learned scholar, but his absolute passion for the subject was remarkable. If he was boyish charm before he was all seriousness now as he listened intently while I related everything I could remember, trying not to leave out a single detail.

He walked a coin across his knuckles as he listened, as if he did not know how to be still or perhaps needed to be moving in order for his brain operate at full efficiency. He asked questions of both myself and Frank, pulling out details we'd forgotten as easily as if he were pulling silk scarves from his sleeve.

"I've heard many stories from the old country, even one actual firsthand account of a sort of were-beast—a hideous, demonic combination of man and animal. Some take the form of a wolf, but it's been said there are other forms as well. Anywhere in the world where men and beast live, they can be found. It is a low, dirty business to become one of these poor, cursed creatures," he said and shuddered." And they are difficult to kill."

"But, it could be done? Is that what you're telling us? We can kill this foul thing?" asked Frank.

"Yes." he said.

I interrupted." Gentlemen, please. As you said Mr. Weisz, this poor soul is cursed. I must inquire in the name of mercy, is there no way to remove this curse short of killing them?"

"I know of no way to cure them. Once you become the beast you lose your soul. As my father, the rabbi used to say, 'you can't un-ring that bell'." He said.

I nodded, resigning myself to the fatal conclusion of our enterprise." What do we need to do?"

Erik considered for a moment." Well, you need some

silver, and it should be blessed by a religious leader—a rabbi, or a priest. Some form of holy man, truly consecrated by the divine."

"I have some silver, but it is hardly blessed. It is simply decorative."

"I know where we have a big chunk of holy silver, though Bill Cody isn't gonna like it. There is a big silver cross on his desk."

I jumped on his revelation, near to yelling "Of course! It was a gift from the pope. It's sure to have been blessed. Frank, you're a genius." I hugged him and kissed his cheek. Armed with knowledge from the Great Houdini our success was certain.

"Blessed silver?" Code said." From where should I obtain blessed silver?'

"Bill, it was my thought that we might use that large silver cross that Pope Leo the Thirteenth gave you. I would imagine that would be a blessing of the highest quality."

"But, but...." Cody stammered." It's worth a fortune! How can I have it melted down into bullets? It is a work of art. Expensive art. Irreplaceable."

"Do you have another source readily available?" I asked. He had no adequate response, so with a great gnashing of teeth he acquiesced and had the blacksmith go to work on the project, producing a sufficient quantity of bullets for Mr. Cody, Frank and myself. Being used to producing custom rounds for our marksmanship demonstrations this was not a difficult feat.

Cody then rounded up a handful of his best cowboy trick riders. Explaining only that there was a wild best roaming the encampment and that it was his plan to attempt to trap and kill it that night. They were to hide in a nearby tent and rope the beast to prevent it from attacking while Cody, Frank and I shot the creature.

My dear Frank, always looking out for my welfare

challenged Cody after the meeting with the cowboys." Bill, how do you propose to lure this creature into this trap?"

"With bait, of course."

Frank shook his head." If you think that I would allow my wife to be tied out like a sacrificial goat you have taken leave of your senses."

I raised my hands and spoke softly so that both my champion and the great hunter would lower their voices in order to hear me out. "Gentlemen, please. I am already a target. This is the best course of action to end the threat. I see no reason why we should discuss it any further. Besides," I said spinning the cylinder of my revolver." We are the best shots in the world armed with magic bullets. What could go wrong?"

Cody received another inquiry from Coughlin that afternoon. It was another innocuous statement about how much he cared for our safety and truly wished we would end this stubborn stand and accept his offer of protection. Was the money truly worth the risk? But for all of us at that point it was a matter of principle. Blood had been shed—blood was due.

That night I made a great show of us attending a function in the city. We dance the evening away and loudly announced our exit. We had the carriage take us to the encampment area and stop to allow us to exit at our tent. As it pulled away I said loudly, "I am so tired, my dear Frank. I must retire for the evening. I do believe that I could sleep through Gabriel's horn I am so exhausted."

"Let's to bed then," Frank agreed. And we entered our tent, drew the flap closed and made sure to blow out the oil lamp.

In the darkness, we armed ourselves and waited. Mr. Cody had earlier entered the tent and was waiting with us. We waited for some hours. Not speaking except in occasional whisper as we did not know the creature's capacity for hearing. The cowboys were bunked quietly in the tent next door. I had no doubt that they were alert and awake as well because Mr. Cody was as fine a judge of character as he was of horseflesh.

It was well past midnight when we heard the first sounds. At first, it seemed we heard the faint whispering sound of a flute, barely carried on the wind. The soft notes just at the edge or perception. Then a rustle, and then the unmistakable snort of a buffalo, close by.

The August air turned inexplicably chilly, and I found I could see my breath. Cody nodded at Frank and me. We knew it was time to act. We readied our weapons, each of us armed with an 1886 Winchester level action rifle. Cody made a silent 3 count and we threw open the tent flap and rushed out.

The beast was enormous. It stood facing the tent entrance a mere twenty feet away. Its eyes were unnatural and glowed like coals from the fires of hell. Its fur was black and had a sheen which reflected the glow of the full moon. Immediately upon seeing the animal we three began to fire upon it. The cowboys poured out of the next-door tent and threw lassos around the beast.

I had fired six rounds when I realized that the bullets were having no affect whatsoever on the creature. Although we saw the rounds make contact, and then bounced off the wooly black fur like peas from a peashooter.

The creature jerked its head to the left and jerked against one of the ropes binding it, sending two cowboys flying. It pulled to right and slung two more. It stepped forward towards us dragon along those cowboys who still held on.

One cowboy rushed forward and managed to rope a front and back leg by bouncing a wide lariat off the ground, then back up and he pulled tight. The beast turned to him with a cold glare and jerked its legs back open wide. They couldn't match its strength.

We quickly ran out of bullets, and the hellish buffalo continued forward, slowly, as if it were relishing our last moments. I have no doubt whatsoever that it was set upon causing my death.

Both Cody and my dear Frank stepped in front of me with the beast a mere three feet away. "Run!" Frank screamed. But I was not about to leave those brave men to die alone.

The beast lifted its head to full height and looked down upon us just before striking. Its eyes literally showed deep, red flame and a smoke of fowl sulfuric brimstone snaked out of its mouth.

Just as it was to strike, I heard a low plaintive voice, and a feathered arrow appeared in its side. I looked to my right and saw that Sitting Bull was singing some Lakota Sioux chant and notching another arrow. He let loose with the second flight and hit the beast again and another feathered shaft protruded from its body.

The buffalo dropped to its front knees and wavered before collapsing on its side. Its breathing became labored and a misty, smoke enveloped its form. In a few moments the buffalo had disappeared and the nude body of an emaciated, ancient Indian woman wearing a tattered buffalo robe was in its place.

Cody walked forward toward the woman. She was not quite dead. "Who are you?"

"The last. You have killed us all now. When you killed the buffalo, we starved. This is a good death. To starve is a horror. I hope you spend eternity in white man's Hell for what you did. I hope Coughlin finds a way to make you suffer."

With those haunting words, she died.

I felt a hand on my shoulder. I turned and looked into the dark eyes of Chief Sitting Bull.

"So, Little Sure Shot," Sitting Bull said. "How come you didn't tell me about this?"

"Mr. Cody didn't want to scare your people."

Sitting Bull laughed. "This is Indian magic; we live with this magic all our lives. You were foolish. Bullets can't hurt such a spirit beast."

"But they were silver bullets, blessed by the pope."

"Ha! White man's magic," he spit on the ground. "Only a point dipped in the white ash of cedar and sage can penetrate the hide of skin walker."

Cody returned to stand with us, leaving the pitiful corpse on the ground with the cowboys gawking in disbelief at what had just occurred.

I think Mr. William Cody later had it right when he said: *"You who live your lives in cities or among peaceful ways cannot always tell whether your friends are the kind who would go through fire for you. But on the Plains one's friends have an opportunity to prove their mettle."*

Well, my dear Frank's and my erstwhile friend Buffalo Bill Cody's mettle was shown that night, and they were not found wanting.

The End

AFTERWORD

We have taken great liberty with reality in this story, but many elements are true.

Susan B. Anthony gave those rousing speeches. Nicolas Tesla had a major showcase through the Westinghouse Company with a model of what was to be the method of electrifying the world with alternating current.

Harry Houdini aka Erik Weisz was indeed performing with his brother Theo aka "Dash" on the midway. Houdini was in fact fascinated with spiritualism and all things occult. In later life he became a great debunker of charlatans, not because he was not a believer but in fact because he wanted to find "true" psychics.

Buffalo Bill had been shunned by the planners of the Exposition and considered too low brow for their classy event. In going it alone and leasing the property adjacent to the midway, he made a fortune that they couldn't touch. They were not happy about the situation at all.

In actuality, the fair would have lost its shirt if not for the addition of George Washington Gale Ferris Jr.'s great steam powered "Ferris Wheel".

Of course the moon cannon is a fiction with a nod to Jules Verne, but if anyone could have pulled it off it would have been Andrew Carnegie. We also give a nod to the travelling Professor Uhrwerk and his automatons from "Tinker's Damn". His experimentation with uranium power supplies derived from the leetso rocks obtained from New Mexico and his advancements in clockwork design made him a star attraction in our version of 1893. (Uhrwerk is based on the German word for clockwork, by the way.)

Lastly, there is one change to our 1893 that some folks might already have realized if they are up on their history of the Old West. Sitting Bull did indeed join the Buffalo Bill Wild West in 1885, and he saw many wonders. He did have an affinity for Annie Oakley and did call her *Watanya*

Cicilla if the hype can be believed. But Sitting Bull did not make it to the Chicago World's Fair.

He became tired and jaded by what he had seen, the vast population of white people, the industrialization of the landscape, the abject poverty compared with the wanton ostentation of the affluent. He was also subjected to the ridicule of the crowd as the demon redskin who had massacred the saintly General George Custer.

He finally said that he would rather "die an Indian than live a white man." He gave up his salary of $50 per week and returned to the Standing Rock Reservation.

In 1889 the Ghost Dance began to sweep the plains. Fearful that Sitting Bull would be a powerful icon, Indian Agency authorities directed Lakota police officers to take him prisoner.

In 1890, the old man was dragged from his cabin and in the ensuing fight was shot in the side and in the head. He was buried at Fort Yates, North Dakota but later exhumed and moved to Mobridge, South Dakota which was near his place of birth.

In our version, Sitting Bull found hope in the new future. That perhaps his people could forge a way forward secure in the knowledge that although the white man may have been technologically superior, they lacked the wisdom required to manage their own greed. Sooner or later the old ways would have to stay alive to help man reclaim his soul.

Bill Allen 2013

ABOUT THE AUTHORS

Bill D. Allen is an Oklahoma writer, motorcyclist and blues enthusiast. He is the author of the novels GODS AND OTHER CHILDREN, SHADOW HEART and the coauthor of PIRATES OF OUTRIGGER RIFT. His website is: *BILLDALLEN.COM*

Sherri Dean is a Kansas City writer and artist. Her latest work is available in the anthologies DEATH IS ONLY SKIN DEEP and I SHOULD HAVE STAYED IN OZ.

Made in the USA
Columbia, SC
25 January 2023